A Fallen Star

by

Gemma Owen-Kendall

To Jayne
Thank you for your
Continued Support.
Best Wishes
Gemma
x

1

About the Author

This book is a new challenge for this author; usually Gemma writes young adult stories about first time love and fantasy. However, Gemma has attempted to create her own poetry that portrays wishes, love, grief and heartbreak. The author currently lives in Grimsby, UK with her partner and her dog Hunnie.

Book Description

A first poetry collection from author Gemma Owen-Kendall. Sometimes, believing to wish upon a star may come true eventually if you never give up. If you want what your heart desires, just wish for it.

Preface

Thank you in advance for giving the chance to read my first ever collection of poems. Poetry isn't something I usually write but over the years from a child up to now, I've had a lot of feelings to express so I've put these into poems.

Acknowledgements

I would like to express my special thanks to all the writers from my local area of North-East Lincolnshire. You've all helped inspire me to write my first ever poetry collection.

Dedication

*To the people I once knew, this book
goes out to you.*

One Day I Will.

One day I will hold your hand and never let go.

One day I will hold you, forever and now.

One day I will be your girl but until then,

I will wait for that one day when we can be whole.

I Never Knew.

I never knew love existed until I met you.

The feeling of never wanting you out of my life.

I never knew love existed until I kissed you.

The feeling of never wanting to stop kissing you.

I never knew love existed until you told me, you loved me first.

The feeling of never wanting to stop loving you torments me.

I never knew love until you showed me how to love you.

The feeling of wanting this with you forever and always.

Love, That Feeling.

Love, that feeling of wanting to share
a life with another.

Love, of knowing it is you I want to
be with.

Love, to me is more than just a
word.

Love, just wanting to share my
emotions with you.

I Only Wish

I only wish to see you once again, to
have those dreamy eyes gazing
back into mine.

I only wish to stroke my hands
through your hair and kiss those
luscious lips of yours.

I only wish to know what fate has
lined up for us, but I guess I will
never know.

I only wish to wonder if I ever cross
your mind, your thoughts or if you've
forgotten all about me.

I only wish upon a falling star to see
you once again.

I only wish when I blew the candle out on my birthday cake to see and speak to you again.

I only wish to just run up to you and wrap my arms around you like nothing ever happened.

I only wish to miss you deeply as you will always have a place in my heart.

Those months we shared were enough to love a lifetime's worth, I only wish to have all this again with you.

I'm On A Journey

I'm on a journey to discover and find myself once again but not the type of travel to go to a new place.

I'm on a journey to be at peace with my emotions a day heartbreak caused by you. The continuous feelings of anxiety and chest pain have slowly eased at bay.

I'm on a journey to forgive you but I know I will never get over you. As you will always have a special place in my heart that I intend to hold dear.

I'm on a journey to be me once again, but I wish for what we had to have never ended. I was and still am so fragile minded to come to grips with what love truly is.

A Shooting Star

That evening, I took a drive in my
car, I glanced up at the starry night
sky.

There it was before my eyes, a
shooting star right there before me
but from afar.

The saying is to wish upon a star, if
only I could catch it in a jar.

The one thing I do want to wish for,
is to have my heart with you.

Quest For Love

Life is sacred and beautiful specially to have you in it, before we spoke I was a lost soul and losing sight for who I was as a person. I've always had this idea on what love is truly like and how it should be, but it's never been there for me. I've been searching for that one person who can whisk me off my feet, take me on a journey of love as well as save me from losing myself. I believe and know that person is you, it's as though the fates have bought us together and now, I don't want to lose sight of you. Without knowing, I have written many stories about you and never realised you would be crafted into a real person. I've longed to have a guy who is dark and mysterious as well as sexy and good looking, now you are finally here and hope you will be the hero of my story on my quest to find love and myself again.

From The Very First Moment

From the very first moment that I saw you, I was always intrigued by you.

From the very first moment that I saw you, I obviously had some hidden desire for you.

From the very first moment that we finally spoke, I never knew how much of an impact I had on you.

From the very first moment that I'd dreamed of you, my hidden desire of you erupted.

From the very first moment that our friendship blossomed, I knew I longed to belong to you.

Starry Night Sky

Oh starry night sky, twinkling above me, sparkling upon this night sky.

Oh starry night sky, please grant me my wishes upon this sparkling night sky.

Oh starry night sky with your dazzling lights, burning above me upon this nightly lit sky.

Please watch over me as you twinkle above me on this starry night sky.

I Remember

I remember the first time we met, I couldn't take my eyes off you.

I remember the first time we spoke, I couldn't get you off my mind.

I remember the first time we kissed, that magical moment I will never forget.

I remember the first time you told me you loved me, this is a memory I hold dear.

Is This Goodbye?

Is this goodbye? I hope its only for now and not forever. I'm struggling to keep my feelings at bay.

Is this goodbye? I hope its not for good. I'm struggling to come to terms with you not being here today.

Is this goodbye? I hope this is not for real. I'm struggling to accept I may have been led astray.

Is this goodbye? Oh please I hope it is not. I'm struggling to be okay as each day passes me by.

My Heart

My heart is not just an organ, a
muscle or a vessel to pump blood
through my arteries around my body.

My heart feels my thoughts and
emotions, it knows what it wants.

My heart is not just a part of my
body fulfilling its daily duties.

My heart feels my strengths and
weaknesses, it takes over my soul. It
is part of my soul.

My heart loves and breaks easily,
the heart can't help who it chooses
to belong too.

My heart chooses to belong to you,
my love.

Crush

How can some small crush transpire
into something more. From just
gazing at you to a rush of fluttering
butterflies in my tummy.

How can some small crush inspirer
into a dream about you. I'm just so
crazy about you, wanting to have
more from you.

How can some small crush fire up
into a love whirl with you. You
fulfilled my every desire leaving me
to crave more of you.

The Mask

Why do you hide behind a persona
of pretending to be someone or
something else. It's as though you
are wearing a mask.

Why do you hide away from me and
yet watch over me from a distance.
It's as though you want to be my
hero but you just hold back.

Why do you hide behind a
camouflage mask, the soft green
cloth covering the lower part of your
face. It's as though you are some
stow away.

Why do you hide away from me your
true self, does the real you ever exist
or is it concealed at bay.

Why do you hide behind your nickname, like a thief? It's as though you always see yourself behind the mask of one.

I Miss You

I miss you so much like the sky
needs the sun.

I miss you so much like the trees
need the leaves.

I miss you so much like the night sky
needs the stars.

I miss you so much like the flowers
need petals.

I miss you so much like the Earth
needs the oceans.

I miss you so very much just like my
heart needs you.

Teenage Dream

To live those moments once again of feeling younger, like a teenager. Not having a care in the world until I saw you. To lock eyes with you and not wanting to look away. Reliving those moments again of first love and innocence, just like a teenager. Even more so is that you're feeling this moment like me. It is as though we are reliving our teenage dreams once again. Sneaking out and meeting up in secluded places where we can't be seen by prying eyes. I hope we can have another teenage dream one day, to have the first touch of the hand, to the first kiss.

I Hate You, I Love You

I hate you, I hate what you've done to me, you've crushed me, you b***ard and now you must pay the price. Over and over in my head I hear you telling me how much you loved me but it was all lies. I let you get into my head and I let you get into my body and now you've just gone off without a trace. Did I ever mean anything to you? I did so much for you, I was prepared to change my entire life to be with you but you asked me to wait. Well I did wait and now you've just disappeared.

Some days I imagine finding you and stabbing you over and over again so you can feel how much you've made me suffer. Every puncture from the blade piercing your heart bit by bit. Blood splattering out as I continue to break your heart like you did with mine. Other days I fantasise about us meeting up again and having make up hugs, feeling your touch once again and kissing those luscious lips of yours. But I can't hurt you like you have me as its not in my nature. I still love you and as much as it hurts, I will no doubt forgive you.

Missing You

It pains me to writer this to you but I have to get this off my chest. It's been nearly a year since I last saw you and we last spoke together. We used to talk, text and phone each other everyday but now we don't talk anymore. You haven't phoned or responded to my couple of messages that I've sent to you. What did I do to deserve this? What did I do for you to suddenly not acknowledge my existence anymore? I was there for you when you wanted to chat and get things from off your chest. I was there for you when you needed money and I was there for you when you felt down.

I still remember everything you told me, that you fell in love with me and that you wanted to be with me. I still remember all the secrets you shared with me and I promised not to tell anyone. I still remember you constantly telling me that you love me all the stars in the sky and more, that you wished, hoped and prayed for one day for us to be together.

You told me that I had a big heart and a lot of love to give. You told me that you had never met anyone like me before. You told me that I was your special girl. You told me that you hoped one day to marry me. You told me always and forever, you and me against the world.

Was I stupid enough to believe you? Yes I believed everything you said and still do. I don't know why but I do. I miss you even when I used to see you everyday. I miss you like the sky misses the sun on a rainy day. I miss you, do you miss me too?

I hate that you've broken me, I hate that you've broken my heart. I hate that I don't hate you and I hate that I don't get to talk to you. I truly hope one day you will come back into my life again. As I hate feeling so broken and I hate missing you so much. Wherever you are and whatever you are doing, know that I still love you. Please come back to me.

Goodbye My Loved One

This poem was first published in Girl In The Red Coat, 2021.

My love, my best friend,

You were taken too soon.

My dove, you gave me wings again,

To feel and love with sweet refrain.

You were there, when I was at my low,

To hold and protect, to take things slow.

You will always have a place in my heart,

A place in my dreams, where never apart,

Enjoying our souls, from a horse and cart.

What will seem forever, apart from you,

My heart will always belong to you.

Thanks!

If you've made it to this page, thank you for sticking with my poetry. I would once again like to thank the writers of North-East Lincolnshire for all of your help, guidance and inspiration. The writers I would like to thank in particular are Pauline Seawards and Grace King, both of these lovely ladies are such an inspiration when it comes to writing poetry so I've taken a leaf out of their books to write my own collection. Finally thank you once again to the writers from The Globe Writers.

Check out these other books from the author:

Girl In The Red Coat - 2021

Halloween Screams - 2021

Innocent Times - 2020

Tales From Lockdown - 2020

Christmas Gifts - 2019

Fish and Freaks - 2018

Monday At Six - 2017

Please leave a review of this on Amazon and the author's facebook page.

Author's social media:

Facebook:
www.facebook.com/innocenttimesauthor

Instagram: @gemma.authorpage

Twitter: @GemOwenKendall

Tiktok: @gemmagridgirl

Printed in Great Britain
by Amazon